A NOTE TO PARENTS

Reading Aloud with Your Child

Research shows that reading books aloud is the single most valuable support parents can provide in helping children learn to read.

- Be a ham! The more enthusiasm you display, the more your child will enjoy the book.
- Run your finger underneath the words as you read to signal that the print carries the story.
- Leave time for examining the illustrations more closely; encourage your child to find things in the pictures.
- Invite your youngster to join in whenever there's a repeated phrase in the text.
- Link up events in the book with similar events in your child's life.
- If your child asks a question, stop and answer it. The book can be a means to learning more about your child's thoughts.

Listening to Your Child Read Aloud

The support of your attention and praise is absolutely crucial to your child's continuing efforts to learn to read.

- If your child is learning to read and asks for a word, give it immediately so that the meaning of the story is not interrupted. DO NOT ask your child to sound out the word.
- On the other hand, if your child initiates the act of sounding out, don't intervene.
- If your child is reading along and makes what is called a miscue, listen for the sense of the miscue. If the word "road" is substituted for the word "street," for instance, no meaning is lost. Don't stop the reading for a correction.
- If the miscue makes no sense (for example, "horse" for "house"), ask your child to reread the sentence because you're not sure you understand what's just been read.
- Above all else, enjoy your child's growing command of print and make sure you give lots of praise. *You are your child's first teacher—and the most important one. Praise from you is critical for further risk-taking and learning.*

— Priscilla Lynch
Ph.D., New York University
Educational Consultant

WARNER BROS. PRESENTS
A LEE RICH/GARY FOSTER PRODUCTION A CHRISTOPHER CAIN FILM "THE AMAZING PANDA ADVENTURE"
STEPHEN LANG YI DING RYAN SLATER MUSIC BY WILLIAM ROSS EXECUTIVE PRODUCER GABRIELLA MARTINELLI
STORY BY JOHN WILCOX & STEVEN ALLDREDGE SCREENPLAY BY JEFF ROTHBERG AND LAURICE ELEHWANY
PRODUCED BY LEE RICH, JOHN WILCOX, GARY FOSTER AND DYLAN SELLERS
DIRECTED BY CHRISTOPHER CAIN

ISBN 0-590-55238-4

12 11 10 9 8 7 6 5 4 3 2 1   5 6 7 8 9/9 0/0

Printed in the U.S.A.   09

First Scholastic printing, August 1995

The Amazing Panda Adventure

Adapted by Grace Kim
From the screenplay by
Jeff Rothberg and Laurice Elehwany
Story by John Wilcox & Steven Alldredge

Hello Reader! — Level 3

SCHOLASTIC INC.

New York Toronto London Auckland Sydney

– CHAPTER 1 –

The forest is full of trees—
evergreen and bamboo.
Flowers are in bloom—
purple, orange, and yellow.
A waterfall fills the forest
with waterfall music.
Monkeys holler.
Pandas bark.
Then the animals are quiet.

Little panda is born.
He is very tiny —
small enough to fit
in his mother's great paw.
His fur is fine and white.
He cannot see yet.

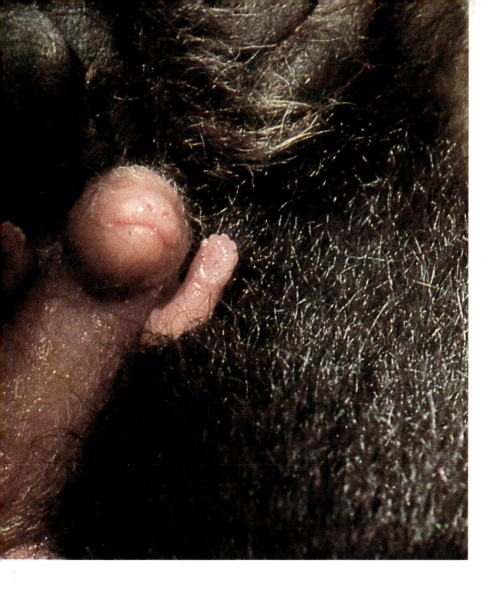

He cannot walk yet.
Mother panda draws him to her heart,
then cradles him in her arms.
Mother panda will feed her baby,
keep him safe,
and watch him grow.

Little panda gets bigger
and bigger.
He is three months old.
His fur is now black
and white.

He can see.
He can walk.
Near the river,
little panda sees
a pretty bird.
She fans shiny
orange feathers.
Little panda must have
a better look.
He walks toward
the pretty bird.
Then he hears a loud bark.
Mother does not want
little panda to stray.
The loud bark
frightens the bird,
and she flies away.
Little panda stretches
his neck to look at
the flying bird.
He loses his balance
and tumbles back
to the edge of the river.

In the water,
he sees another little panda.
He tries to touch it.
Little panda makes ripples
across the water.
How wonderful!
Little panda slaps the water.
Splash!
Little panda splashes again.
What fun!
Then he feels a gentle tug
on his neck.
It is mother panda.
The fun is over.
It is time to go.

Mother panda looks
for lunch.
She gathers bamboo
to eat.
Mother panda's teeth
are large and sharp.
Her jaw is strong.
She chews the
tough bamboo.
Little panda still drinks milk.
He cannot eat food yet.
Mother panda catches
an interesting smell.
It is dried meat,
sweet and salty.
Mother panda squeezes
through thick bushes
to get it.
Suddenly a large door falls.
Mother panda is trapped.
She barks a warning
to little panda.

Little panda runs up a tree to hide.
He watches and waits in fear.
Mother panda is silent and still,
as if she is asleep.
A group of humans surrounds her.
Little panda does not understand
what they are doing.
They touch her eyes and her ears.
They stroke her fur.
The humans are scientists.
They study animals.
They try to help the pandas
in the forest.
The scientists put something
on mother panda's neck.
It is a pretty blinking thing.
Now they will always be able
to find mother panda.
Then they go away.
Little panda climbs down the tree.
He licks mother's paw
and it moves.
Mother panda is awake.

– Chapter 2 –

Little panda is growing
every day.
And every day
he sees new things.
When mother is busy
gathering bamboo,
little panda has time
to learn and explore.
A beautiful butterfly
visits little panda.
He holds out a paw
to touch it,
but it flutters away—
just out of reach.
Little panda and the butterfly
play a happy game of chase.

But little panda strays too far.
Mother panda barks,
as if to say,
"Come back here!"
She runs after little panda.
Suddenly, a wire trap closes
around her paw.
Mother panda is in pain
and she is afraid.
Danger is near.
She can hear it.
Now she can see it, too.
A leopard is stalking little panda.
But mother panda cannot run.
She cannot protect her cub.

Suddenly, a gunshot rings
through the forest.
The leopard runs away.
But the pandas are not safe.
Two humans come with guns.
One human puts little panda
into a sack.
The other points his gun
at mother panda.
They are poachers.
They kill pandas and sell the furs.
They take cubs from panda mothers
and sell them to zoos.

A third human comes and shouts,
"Don't shoot!"
He wants to save mother panda.
He is a scientist.
Mother panda's blinking collar
has led him to her.
A second shot is fired.
The scientist is shot.
The poachers run away
and take little panda with them.
More humans come.
They help the scientist
and mother panda, too.
They take her up in a helicopter.

In another part of the forest,
little panda sees the helicopter.
He does not know
that it carries his mother.
The poachers take little panda
to a cave
and put him in a basket.
It is dark.
Little panda is hungry.
He needs his mother.
Where could she be?
Little panda waits and waits.
Then he falls asleep.

Strange noises wake little panda.
Suddenly, his basket falls over.
Little panda is afraid.
He sees three humans.
Do they know where his mother is?
She has been gone a long time.

The humans take little panda
from the cave.
They are very kind to him,
not like the other humans
who try to hurt pandas for money.

The humans walk with little panda
for a while.
Then they rest.
Little panda explores the forest.
He notices a bamboo shoot.
It is wiggling and waving at him.
Little panda tries to sniff
the bamboo,
but it disappears into the ground!
Two more bamboo shoots wave
from the ground.
Each time,
little panda tries
to catch the bamboo with his paws.
But each time,
the bamboo disappears.
A bamboo rat is stealing the shoots
from underground.
The humans laugh.
This is a fun game!

Soon they are off again.
They must hurry.
The poachers are chasing them.
The poachers want
the panda cub.
Little panda and his human friends
come to a bridge.
They must cross it.
The poachers are close behind.
But the bridge is breaking.
Little panda falls with the others
into the water below!

Little panda swims and swims.
Finally, he reaches the shore.
His friends are there, too.
Little panda is very hungry.
He is feeling weak.

Chapter 3

In another part of the forest,
mother panda waits, too.
She is in a cage,
away from her cub.
Like little panda,
she is weak.

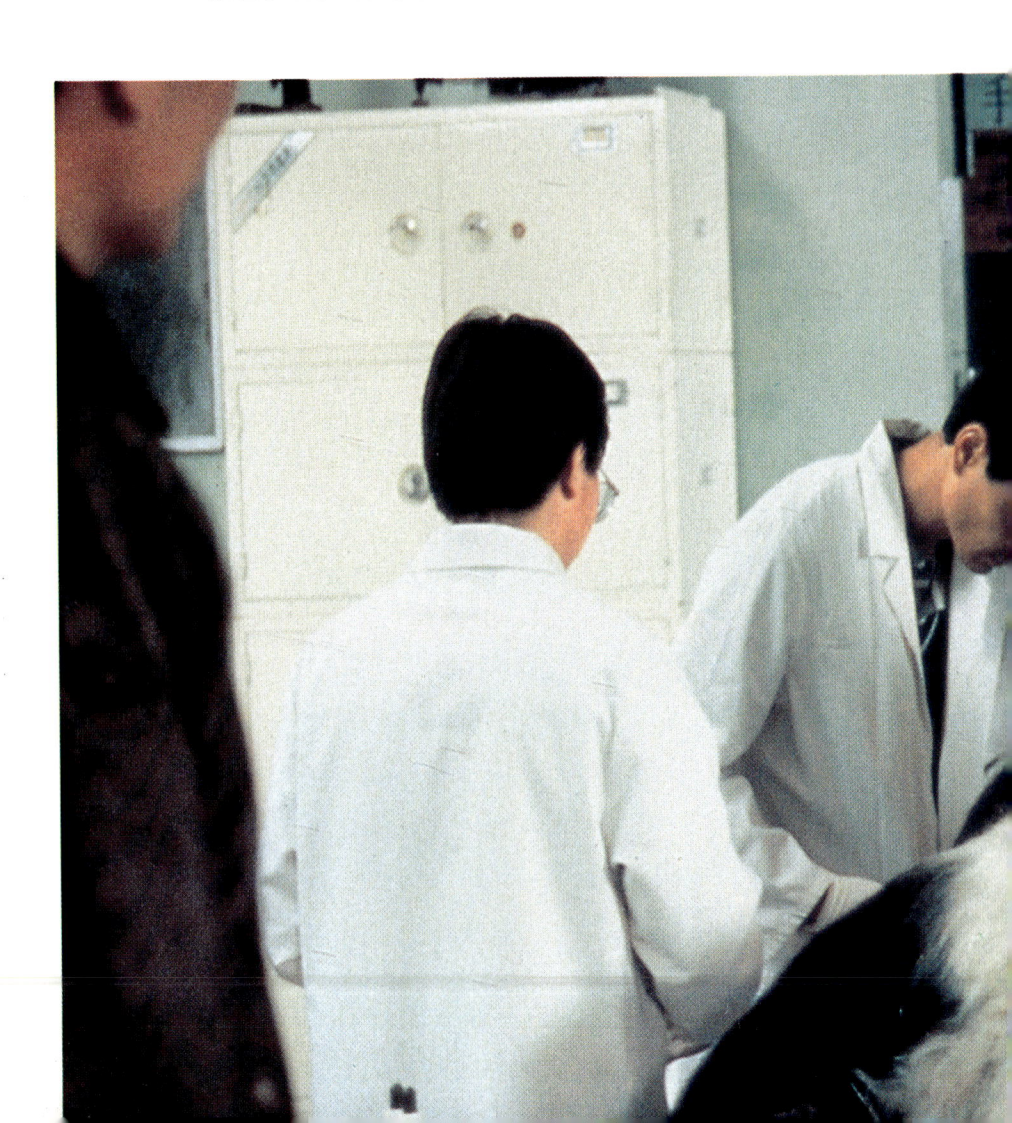

She is too sad to eat.
The humans are kind to her.
They try to heal mother panda's paw.
But mother panda is still very sad.
She is worried about her cub.
Mother panda barks.
She hopes her cub
can hear her.

But he cannot.
He is far away,
deep in the forest.
He and the humans walk
for a long time.
Little panda is getting weaker.
He must have his mother's
milk or he will die.
Danger is very near.
Little panda and his
human friends reach
the edge of a mountain.
The poachers are
on the mountain, too.
Little panda's friends protect him.
The scientist comes to help.
They capture the poachers.
The poachers will no longer
be able to hurt pandas.

His human friends drive
little panda very quickly
through the forest.
They stop.
Little panda sees a building
and more humans.

Then he sees a cage.
Mother panda is there!
She pulls little panda to her
and cradles him in her arms.

As he drinks his mother's milk,
mother panda barks a happy bark.

Her little panda is
safe at last.